When 10-year-old Ben Tennyson stumbles upon a mysterious alien device in the woods one summer, little does he realise that his life is set to change - forever.

As soon as the watch-like Omnitrix quite literally gets a grip on him, Ben discovers it gives him the ability to transform into 10 different alien super-beings, each one with awesome powers!

Using the Omnitrix to cause super-powered mischief turns out to be fun, but will Ben learn to use his might to fight for good?

READ ON AND FIND OUT . . .

EGMONT

We bring stories to life

Published in Great Britain 2009
by Egmont UK Limited
239 Kensington High Street, London W8 6SA

Ben 10 and all related characters and elements
are trademarks of and © Cartoon Network.
(s09)

Adapted from the animated series by
Barry Hutchison

1 3 5 7 9 10 8 6 4 2

A CIP catalogue record for this title is available from
the British Library

Printed and bound in Great Britain by the CPI Group

CHAPTER ONE

THE BIG APPLE

The skyscrapers of New York City stretched high above Ben, Grandpa and Gwen as they passed through the entrance of a large hotel. The cousins were excited – they had been sleeping in The Rust Bucket for weeks, but now they were about to book into an actual hotel!

And not just *any* hotel. It was the most luxurious-looking hotel either of them had ever seen. What's more, if the lobby were anything to go by, it was the biggest one they'd ever seen too!

While Grandpa Max spoke with the woman at the check-in desk, Gwen looked through the building's brochure. With every word she read she became more and more excited.

'Wow, this hotel has everything!' she said. 'Indoor pool, spa . . .'

'Now, don't get used to it,' warned Grandpa. 'It's only for one night.'

They picked up their suitcases and began to wheel them across the lobby. Before they were even halfway across, Ben stopped. Something had caught his attention. Something amazing!

'Whoa!' he cried, dropping his case. A sign hanging above a nearby door showed one of the characters from *Sumo Slammers*, Ben's favourite TV show.

Ben ran towards the door. The latest video game based on the show wasn't out for months, but a sneak preview was taking place on the other side of that door. He had to get in – nothing was going to stop him!

A large security guard stopped him. He

loomed above Ben, muscles bulging under his
black suit.

'Pass?' he growled.

Ben pretended to search through his
pockets. 'Must've left it inside,' he smiled. 'I'm
one of the game pros testing out the system.'

Ben grinned confidently and folded
his arms. The guard would definitely fall for
that one.

'VIPs only.'

OK, so maybe he wouldn't fall for it. Ben

turned and slunk back to Grandpa and Gwen with his head hung low.

'I know what you're thinking,' Grandpa Max whispered. 'So no sneaking back in there.'

'I won't,' Ben sighed. He hung back, watching Grandpa and Gwen drag their bags across to the elevator. *He* wouldn't sneak in, but he knew an alien who would!

After a quick check to make sure no one was watching, Ben activated the Omnitrix. A cloud of energy swirled over him, transforming him into the terrifying Ghostfreak!

Making himself invisible, Ghostfreak floated silently past the security guard and through the closed doors.

The room he emerged into was *Sumo Slammers* heaven! Posters and cardboard cut-outs of the characters lined the walls. Ghostfreak barely even noticed. Instead he floated straight for a games console that was set up in the middle of the room.

'The ultimate sneak peek,' he whispered, picking up a controller, 'for the ghost with the most freak!'

✖ ✖ ✖

Out in the lobby, Grandpa and Gwen paused at the elevator. Something was wrong. Something was missing . . .

'Ben?' said Grandpa. He turned round and sighed. Ben was nowhere to be seen.

✖ ✖ ✖

'Yes!' Ben cheered. 'New high score!'

On screen, a huge sumo wrestler performed a dance of celebration. Over Ben's shoulder, an equally large shape slowly stepped forwards.

'What've you got to say for yourself, kid?' snarled the security guard.

Ben looked down at the Omnitrix and

gasped. In the excitement of playing, he hadn't noticed the transformation wearing off. He was no longer Ghostfreak, which meant he was no longer invisible.

He looked up at the guard and smiled nervously. 'Ah . . . "game over"?'

✖ ✖ ✖

Grandpa's suitcase hit the pavement with a thud. He looked down at it sadly.

'And never come back!' warned the

security guard. He growled at Ben one more time before pushing his way back into the hotel.

Grandpa, Ben and Gwen all bent down together and picked up their cases. The wheels squeaked as they pulled them along the street in the direction of The Rust Bucket.

'I told you not to sneak in there!' said Grandpa.

'Well, if you want to get all "technical" about it!'

'I never even got a chance to take a shower!' complained Gwen. 'In a *real* shower, for the first time all summer. Plus they had a spa! A *spa*!' She sighed and turned away from her cousin. 'Nice going, doofus.'

They arrived at The Rust Bucket and clambered inside. It felt even smaller now than it usually did.

'How do you expect me to trust you if you keep misusing the watch?' Grandpa asked.

'Excuse me! I've used it a hundred times

for good,' Ben protested. 'Why can't I use it just once for me?'

'It's not how *many* times you use it, Ben, it's *how* you use it.'

Ben shrugged. 'It was no big deal.'

'To you. And that's all you care about,' glowered Grandpa. 'So no more *Sumo Slammers* stuff for two weeks. No comics, no trading cards . . .'

'No fair!' cried Ben.

'Neither's getting booted from a four-star hotel I already paid for!'

'Fine. Take it out of my allowance!'

'You don't get an allowance,' Gwen reminded him.

'Stay out of this!' snapped Ben and Grandpa together.

Ben scowled. 'This is my vacation too! You can't always tell me what to do. You're not my dad.'

'Well, if I were . . .' Grandpa began. He

stopped and shook his head. Arguing was getting them nowhere. 'Look, I'm going back in the hotel to see if I can get at least some of my money back,' he said. 'I'll be back in a few minutes.'

'Don't hurry,' muttered Ben. He stormed off to the back of The Rust Bucket and pulled the dividing door over with a slam.

'He'll be fine,' Gwen told Grandpa. He nodded, then climbed out of the motorhome and headed back towards the hotel.

'Not fair! Not fair! Totally not fair!' moaned Ben. He kicked the thin door, making it shake.

'Glad to hear you're handling things so maturely,' said Gwen as Ben slid the door open again. He pushed past her, making his way towards the exit. 'Where do you think you're going?' she demanded.

'Where does it look like? Out.'

He jumped down from The Rust Bucket and marched off along the street, away from the hotel. Gwen hopped down after him.

'Get back here!'

'Sorry,' Ben snapped. 'I don't speak dweeb.'

Gwen watched him walk away, then decided to follow. There was no saying what he'd get up to if he were left on his own. 'You,' she sighed, 'are going to be so grounded!'

After a few twists and turns, Ben rounded a corner and found himself standing outside a video arcade called 'The Total Zone'. He smiled. This would be the perfect place to chill out.

He ducked through the doorway and into the arcade. Gwen paused outside, listening to the bleeping, beeping and chiming of hundreds of video games. She shook her head.

'Next summer,' she sighed, 'I'm going to sleep-away camp.'

CHAPTER TWO

A NEW FRIEND?

*B*en wandered through The Total Zone with eyes as wide as saucers. Everywhere he looked he saw something unbelievably cool. Every type of games machine he could think of was in this place, and the only problem he had was deciding which one to try first.

At last, he settled on a baseball simulator. He stepped on to the sensor plate, picked up the bat and dropped his coins into the slot. On the monitor, an animated pitcher stepped up and prepared to throw the ball.

Ben tightened his grip on the bat, getting ready to knock the ball out of the on-screen park. As the pitcher wound up his arm to throw, the picture shuddered and then froze. Ben watched with horror as the words 'Game Over' flashed up on the screen.

'Game over?' He frowned. 'It just started.' He spotted an attendant strolling past. 'This thing just ate my tokens!' he complained.

'Read the sign, kid,' shrugged the attendant. 'It says "Play at your own risk".'

"This place is a rip off! Know that?!'

Over by another machine, a boy with long black hair watched on with interest.

'You're right,' he said. 'The games here stink.'

'Yeah, but not as bad as his breath,' said Ben, still watching the attendant. '*Major* case of sewer mouth.'

The boy laughed. 'You're funny,' he smiled. 'Here. You owe me one.'

He rested a hand on one of the machines. A wave of blue energy crackled from his fingertips. Almost at once, hundreds of tokens

poured out from inside the cabinet.

'*Whoa!* How'd you do that?'

'I've got some skills.'

Ben bent down and scooped up handfuls of the shiny tokens. There were enough here to keep him playing for months!

'We can't take those,' said Gwen, suddenly appearing behind him. 'They're not ours.'

'They are now,' Ben replied. 'Thanks,' he said to the boy. 'I'm Ben.'

'Kevin.'

'Wanna play some air hockey?'

Kevin opened his mouth to say 'yes', then closed it again. Four teenagers were pushing their way through the crowds in his direction.

'Nuh. Gotta bail,' Kevin said. He turned and walked away quickly.

'He's total trouble,' Gwen warned.

'He seemed OK to me,' replied Ben, before one of the gang members shoved him out of the way. He watched them close in on Kevin. His new friend was in trouble.

'Long time no see,' snarled an evil-looking thug as he stepped out in front of Kevin. 'Where you going, freak? Home to recharge your batteries?'

Kevin backed away, but two other gang members caught him by the arms and held him in place. He was trapped!

'Need some help?' asked Ben.

'Huh,' scoffed the leader. 'He's going

to need a lot more than you. Now beat it.' He pushed Ben hard in the chest, sending him tumbling backwards on to the ground.

Ben leaped back to his feet. 'I've got some skills too,' he muttered.

Ducking behind another arcade cabinet, he gave the Omnitrix's dials a twist. He wanted to take care of these thugs quickly, and when it came to doing things quickly, there was one alien he could always rely on.

'So how's the hangout?' Kevin sneered at the gang leader. 'Still trashed like I left it for you?'

'Yeah, and you're gonna pay! You can't take us all alone, freak!'

'But *I* can!'

A strange figure stepped from behind an arcade machine. Ben had transformed into the ultra-fast XLR8!

'Little early for Halloween, dude, isn't it?' cackled one of the gang members.

In a blinding blur of speed, XLR8 shot towards the group. He circled them, running faster and faster, until the gang leader was lifted off the ground by a mini tornado. He screamed as the whirlwind spun him round and round.

As suddenly as he had started, XLR8 stopped. The gang leader hung in the air for a second, frantically flapping his arms in an attempt to stop himself falling.

It was no use. His screams continued as he dropped like a stone back towards the arcade floor. Just before he hit, XLR8 flicked out his tail. It struck the thug on the side and slammed him hard against the nearest wall. He let out a low groan as he slid slowly to the ground.

XLR8 shot off around the arcade. The gang members tried to follow him with their eyes, but the alien was far too fast.

'Where'd he go?' whimpered one of them. A streak of speed lifted him off his feet and

crunched him down on top of the gang's boss.
Another of the thugs quickly found himself
hurtling headlong towards the pile. Then
another, and another.

In the blink of an eye, all five members of
the gang were stacked up against a wall. They
groaned quietly, not sure what had hit them,
but certain they didn't want it to happen again.

XLR8 screeched to a halt next to Kevin.
He fired off a friendly salute, and then rocketed
away to find cover before the transformation
wore off.

※ ※ ※

A few minutes later, Gwen joined Ben outside
The Total Zone. She scowled at him, her hands
on her hips.

'I can't believe you went alien!'

'He helped me, so I helped him. You
wouldn't get it. And neither would Grandpa,'

Ben snapped. 'That's the problem.'

'You see what that speed guy di
losers?' cried Kevin, emerging from insi
arcade.

'Yeah,' Ben smiled. 'Dude's name is XLR8.
In fact, we're pretty tight.'

'Cool! Hey, want a tour of New York?'

'You keep Grandpa waiting any longer
he's going to pop another gasket. We gotta go.'
Gwen stared at her cousin through narrowed
eyes. 'Like *now*, Ben.'

Ben snorted. 'Don't you mean *you* have to
go?'

Gwen shook her head, but realised there
was nothing she could say that would change
his mind. 'You're on your own,' she sighed,
walking off.

'Good. That's the way I want it.' Ben
turned his back on his cousin and followed
Kevin through the back streets of New York
City.

'So how'd you get your power?' Ben asked after a while.

'I was born with it,' Kevin explained. 'I'm like an energy sponge. Motors, air conditioners, lights, batteries, whatever. Soak it up, then dish it out when I have to.' He grinned wickedly. 'Or want to.'

'Cool!'

'Come on,' said Kevin. 'I'll show you where I live.'

He led Ben through unfamiliar streets and alleyways until they reached a boarded-up entrance to an old subway station. Kevin pulled a plank of wood to the side, making room for Ben to squeeze through.

The station had been abandoned for years, but for Kevin it was home. Broken furniture lay scattered about, alongside some high-tech TV and computer game equipment. A huge *Sumo Slammers* cut-out stood guard next to the gadgets. Ben thought it may well have been the coolest place he had ever s

'You live here?' asked Ben.

'Yeah, by myself.'

'What about your family?'

'Long gone.' Kevin shrugged. 'They weren't too thrilled at having a freak for a son. But it just means I don't answer to nobody.'

'Sounds good to me. So why was that gang after you?'

'I kinda trashed their hangout under the Thirty-Ninth Street bridge,' explained Kevin. 'What about you? Sounds like your grandpa's pretty steamed at you.'

'Like usual,' Ben sighed. 'And all I did was sneak in and play the new *Sumo Slammers* computer game.'

'The one that won't be out until Christmas?' Kevin asked.

'Yeah.'

Kevin's mouth curled into a grin. He had an idea!

'I got a tip a new shipment just came in,'
whispered Kevin. He had led Ben down to the
docks, and now they were crouching in the
shadows outside an old warehouse.

After checking the coast was clear, Kevin
sneaked up to the door. It was locked. An
electronic keypad was mounted on the wall next
to it. Any normal person would need a code to
get inside, but then Kevin wasn't any normal
person.

The keypad sparked and fizzled as Kevin
held his hand over it. With a **CLUNK** the lock
slid open, and the two boys stepped into the
warehouse. Neither of them noticed the light of
a security alarm begin to blink as they entered.

Rows and rows of wooden boxes were
stacked up inside the warehouse. Kevin walked
over to one and prised the lid open. With a flick

of his wrist, he tossed Ben a copy of the brand-new *Sumo Slammers* game.

'Check it out! Wait's over, dude,' Kevin grinned.

'Yesss!' cheered Ben, before the sound of shattering glass caught his attention. He looked up in time to see four metal cylinders come crashing through the windows. Even before they hit the ground, the canisters had begun to spray clouds of choking tear gas everywhere.

With a screeching of tyres and blaring of sirens, a squad of police cars skidded to a stop outside the warehouse. Overhead, Ben could hear helicopters swooping closer. His stomach tightened into a knot as he realised that he and Kevin were completely surrounded!

CHAPTER THREE

SHOO, FLY, SHOO!

Ben coughed. The tear gas was filling the warehouse. They didn't have much time.

'What do we do?' he wheezed.

'Get outta here!'

They ran. Spotting a power socket, Kevin stopped. He touched the outlet and a surge of energy shot along his arm. The warehouse was lit by a bright blue light as Kevin drained all the power he needed.

A set of wide double doors exploded inwards, and two policemen came running in. They both wore masks to protect them from the gas, and each one held a powerful rifle.

'Freeze, punks!' they yelled.

Kevin clambered up into the driver's seat of a forklift truck. For a moment, his hand glowed with energy. The forklift spluttered, then roared into life.

'Time to rev things up!'

With a wave of his hand, Kevin sent the forklift speeding forwards. It trapped the policemen against a stack of wooden crates.

'Let's go!' Kevin cried. He and Ben sprinted to the exit, only for a police car to block the way. They ran in the other direction, but another car pulled up in front of them.

'Great,' groaned Ben as they both ducked behind a large crate. 'No way out.'

'Any ideas?' asked Kevin.

Ben glanced down at the watch. He knew he shouldn't do this, but . . .

'Only one,' he said. 'But can you keep a secret?'

'Sure.'

Ben twisted the dial on the Omnitrix,

searching for the one alien he knew could get them out of this mess.

'What are you doing with your watch?' Kevin frowned.

Ben didn't answer. Instead, he slammed his hand, triggering another transformation.

Energy swirled out from the watch and began to change him.

Four antennae eyes pushed out from the side of his head, just as an extra pair of legs sprouted from his hips. Huge insect wings burst out from his back, completing the transformation. Ben had become the alien Stinkfly.

'Uh! You reek!' Kevin winced.

'I know!'

Outside, a dozen policemen edged towards the doors. They were sent tumbling like skittles as a green shape shot straight through the middle of them. Helplessly, they watched it soar off across the water.

❈ ❈ ❈

Stinkfly swooped down low over the waves, carrying Kevin below him. The boy could hardly believe what was happening.

'Oh, yeah! And people call *me* a freak. How'd you do that?'

'Talk later,' hissed Stinkfly. He'd spotted a squadron of police helicopters close behind.

The alien insect dodged just in time to avoid a sudden burst of machine-gun fire.

Stinkfly banked upwards, trying to shake off their pursuers. He zoomed up towards the Statue of Liberty, which towered above the New York harbour.

Two of the police helicopters swung round the statue's left side. They met the third, which had flown round on the right. Their target was nowhere to be seen.

'Where'd they go?' barked one of the pilots.

Down below one of the helicopters, Stinkfly and Kevin clung tightly on. If they moved, they would be seen, but they didn't have much choice.

'I'm running out of time,' Stinkfly warned. 'I'll lose them in the city.'

Catching hold of Kevin, Stinkfly dropped down from the underside of the helicopter. The rat-tat-tat of machine-gun fire followed him as he sped down towards New York.

The helicopters were quickly catching up. Stinkfly kept as low to the ground as he could, dodging in and out of traffic, making things as difficult as possible for the pilots. They wouldn't dare open fire in such a crowded place.

A spray of bullets ricocheted off the road just a few metres from Stinkfly's head. The police weren't holding back. They were shooting to kill!

Zipping left and right, Stinkfly weaved his way through the city streets. No matter which way he turned, the helicopters followed. No matter how fast he flew, they got steadily closer.

This was bad. *Really* bad.

Stinkfly didn't notice The Rust Bucket as he swooped over the top of it, but Gwen and Grandpa noticed him – and the helicopters chasing him. They watched in horror until he flew round a corner and out of sight.

'Can't shake 'em!' Stinkfly gasped. The three helicopters had rounded the bend behind him, and were lining up their next shots. He spotted a huge car transporter about to drive under a road bridge below. 'I've got an idea,' he buzzed.

All three pilots watched the insect fly down towards the transporter. It was too close to the bridge for them to get in front of it. They'd catch it on the other side.

When the truck drove out from under the bridge, there was no sign of the creature they had been chasing. Instead, two boys sat in one of the cars, enjoying the ride.

'Where'd that thing go?' demanded a
pilot. The others could only scratch their heads.
Whatever that monster was, it had somehow
managed to get away.

✵ ✵ ✵

A little later, Ben walked along a dirty alleyway,
with Kevin bouncing excitedly at his side.

'So that watch lets you be that dragonfly thing whenever you want?' he quizzed.

'And not just that one,' boasted Ben. 'It sends out this special energy so I can turn into ten different aliens.'

'*Ten?* So the speed guy at the arcade was you?' He pointed at Ben and grinned. 'You're the man! Show me what other aliens you can morph into.'

'It's not that simple.' Ben shrugged. 'It has a mind of its own.'

'Gimme it,' Kevin demanded. 'Maybe I can make it work.'

'Can't. It's stuck on my wrist.'

Kevin stared at the watch for a few moments before a thought occurred to him.

'We should be partners,' he said. 'Between the two of us, with our powers, we could do what we want, whenever we want. I mean totally cash in. What do you say? Huh?' He held his hand out to Ben. 'Friends?'

Ben hesitated, but then took hold of Kevin's hand and gave it a shake. 'Friends,' he said with a nod.

❈ ❈ ❈

The Rust Bucket sped through the streets of the city, dodging in and out of traffic. On board, Gwen held on to her seat as Grandpa pushed the accelerator pedal hard against the floor.

'Of all the stunts Ben's pulled, this is the worst,' Grandpa growled. 'When I find him . . .'

Gwen gulped. She'd never seen her grandfather quite this mad before. She wouldn't like to be in Ben's shoes when they caught up with him.

'I should really be enjoying this,' she sighed. 'So why aren't I?'

❈ ❈ ❈

Kevin and Ben hopped over a gate and landed on the platform of an empty subway station. It looked almost exactly like the one Kevin lived in, except it was much cleaner. The lights dangling down from overhead were all switched on, meaning the station was still in regular use.

'Gimme a boost,' said Kevin, looking up at one of the lights. 'I need to recharge.'

Ben took hold of his friend's foot and lifted him towards the light fitting. Blue waves of energy washed over Kevin as he soaked up the electrical power.

Once he was fully charged, Kevin hopped down on to the tracks and crossed to a lever that stuck up from the ground. As he took hold of the handle, a bolt of energy passed along it. A section of track slowly rotated. It locked into a new position with a **CLANK**.

'What are we doing?' asked Ben.

'A money train loaded with cash comes down this track,' explained Kevin excitedly.

'So when it crashes into the oncoming passenger train – **BOOM!** – instant jackpot! You turn into that XLR8 guy and we're outta here!'

Ben gasped. He couldn't believe what he was hearing. 'But hundreds of innocent people will be killed!'

Kevin's face broke into a wide, wicked grin. 'Hey,' he cackled, 'no pain, no gain!'

CHAPTER FOUR

FRIENDS NO MORE

'You can't do this!' cried Ben.

'Sure we can,' Kevin replied. 'I just switched the tracks!'

Ben bunched his hands into fists. 'I mean, I'm not gonna let you do this.'

'We shook,' snarled Kevin. 'We're partners.'

'No. This is going way too far.'

'Then try and stop me, watch-boy.'

Ben paused, remembering something his Grandpa had said to him. 'You don't care about anyone but yourself,' he whispered.

'You talking about me?' demanded Kevin.

'No,' said Ben. 'I'm talking about me.'

A flash of energy suddenly struck him in the chest. Ben stumbled and tripped over the raised train track.

'You do *not* want to make me mad,' warned Kevin. Coils of energy curled around his hands and flickered along his fingers.

'Me neither,' growled Ben. 'I'm switching the track back.' He gave the Omnitrix a twist. 'Time to go Four Arms!'

With a blinding flash, Ben's transformation began. Something was wrong,

though. He wasn't changing into the super-strong Four Arms after all. Instead, he felt his whole body ignite into a ball of flame as he became Heatblast.

'Stupid watch,' he mumbled. He realised Kevin had seen the entire transformation. 'Move back,' Heatblast commanded.

'Or what? You're going to burn my dinner?'

'Fight me – you're the one who's gonna be burned.'

Kevin threw out an arm and sent electrical energy crackling into the station's power grid. With a series of pops, the overhead lights exploded one by one, plunging the area into near darkness.

Only Heatblast was visible in the gloom. His flames lit him up like a firefly, making him an easy target. Frantically, he looked around for Kevin, but the boy was nowhere to be seen.

A pair of arms wrapped tightly round

Heatblast's neck from behind. Kevin clung on, cackling with delight. It didn't last long. A burst of fiery energy shot up his arm, making him cry out in pain. He dropped from the alien's back and rolled clumsily to safety.

Heatblast spun round, searching for Kevin. Even though Kevin had attacked him, he still felt bad for burning him. Something shone brightly in the nearby shadows and Heatblast stepped closer to take a look.

A ball of spinning flame hit him in the chest, knocking him over as if he were a skittle. The alien lay on the ground for a moment, catching his breath.

He gasped as something that wasn't quite Kevin stepped from the darkness. Much of the villain looked the same as ever, but his head and one arm now looked exactly like Heatblast himself!

Kevin laughed. 'I absorb energy, remember?'

'You don't have to do this!' said Heatblast, leaping to his feet. He threw himself at Kevin, but the boy was too fast. As Heatblast stumbled past, Kevin struck him on the back with another fireball, sending him crashing on to the tracks.

'It's time I got what's coming to me,' cried Kevin. 'No one's calling me "freak" any more!'

Down on the ground, Heatblast wasn't listening. His muscles ached and his head was spinning; Kevin's energy drain had taken a lot out of him.

He was about to pull himself up when he heard a rumble in the distance. It was low and quiet, but getting steadily louder. A light appeared down one of the tunnels. A train was coming.

Heatblast whipped his head round as another sound echoed from the tunnel in the opposite direction. A second light sliced through the dark. Kevin had been right – the trains were going to crash!

The flames behind Kevin's eyes lit up even brighter when he spotted the speeding trains. 'Payday!' he grinned.

Heatblast knew he only had one chance. Reaching out an arm, he launched a jet of flame at the handle, switching the tracks. The fire made the metal glow white-hot. The trains were almost upon him though. Would there be enough time?

A split second before the trains collided, the lever melted, switching the tracks back to their original position. Heatblast felt a wind whip at him as the passenger train sped harmlessly past. He let out a sigh of relief.

He'd saved the day!

But his happiness was short-lived; a horn blasted behind him and he turned round. The money train was speeding straight for him! A tower of flame erupted from the alien before the train thundered across the spot where he had stood.

Kevin watched a wall of fire lick at the front of the train for a few moments, before it faded away. He looked around, but Ben was nowhere to be seen. The train must have finished him off.

So the plan to derail the money train had failed. All that cash: gone. Kevin was disappointed, but he tried to put it from his mind for the moment.

'Forget the money,' he hissed, leaping over the gate that led to the exit. 'Time to get some priceless revenge.'

The money train hurtled along the tracks, trying to make up for lost time. On board, the driver tried not to think too much about the flaming figure he'd seen standing in the middle of the tracks. It had been a trick of the light, that was all. Nothing to worry about.

Meanwhile, less than a metre above the driver's head, Heatblast clung on to the train's shiny metal roof. His fiery fingers slid on the slippery surface. The wind whooshed past, making it difficult to keep his eyes open, and threatening to blow out his flame. His grip slipped on the roof and he skidded back along the train.

He bounced hard on the last carriage and felt the roof slip past beneath him. Instinctively, he blasted the metal with a mini fireball, creating a hole just the right size for his hand. Heatblast forced his fingers inside and held on for all he was worth.

Now he had a handhold he could relax.
In his alien form he was strong enough to keep
his grip, and there was bound to be a station
coming up soon. The train would stop and he
would hop off. What could possibly go wrong?

BLEEP BLEEP BLEEP BLEEEEP! The
watch flashed a worrying shade of red. Realising
what was about to happen, Heatblast sighed.

'Oh, man, I hate that sound!'

✖ ✖ ✖

The Rust Bucket skidded round a bend,
narrowly avoiding crashing into a hotdog stand.
In the passenger seat, Gwen fiddled with the
short-range radio, trying to pick up emergency-
service broadcasts. With a crackle of static, they
began receiving a transmission.

'. . . and expect delays on the uptown
subway lines near Fifty-First Street,' warned
the announcer. 'There have been reports of fires

breaking out all over the tunnels.'

'Grandpa!' Gwen gasped.

Grandpa Max nodded and spun the wheel. 'I know!'

�֎ ✖ ✖

On top of the train, Ben was finding it more and more difficult to hang on. The track had emerged from underground and was now travelling on a raised bridge alongside the city streets. The speed and strength of the wind in his face almost choked him. Its icy chill nipped at his knuckles, forcing him to loosen his grip. Any moment now he was going to slip.

The honking of a horn caught his attention. The Rust Bucket was speeding along beside the train. As Ben watched, a soft shade canopy extended from the side of the motorhome. If he could land on that, he'd be safe.

Ben took a deep breath and got ready to leap. He'd only have one chance. If he missed, then . . .

He shook his head. Missing wasn't an option.

Closing his eyes and gritting his teeth, Ben let go of his handhold – and jumped.

CHAPTER FIVE

SIX ARMS ARE BETTER THAN FOUR

With a grunt, Ben thudded against the canopy. He was thrown around wildly, and for a moment he thought he was going to bounce right off. Gradually, The Rust Bucket slowed down, and Ben was able to get a better grip.

'None of this would have happened if you'd just obeyed me from the beginning!' snapped Grandpa, when Ben was back inside the motorhome. 'It's all about trust.'

'Then trust me that Kevin's probably misusing Heatblast's power right now!' replied Ben.

'OK,' Grandpa sighed, 'so where is he?'

Ben thought hard. What did he know about Kevin? Where would he go? What would he –? Of course!

'I think I know,' said Ben gravely. He turned the Omnitrix's dial. 'Going Stinkfly. See you at the Thirty-Ninth Street bridge!'

With a flash of energy, Ben transformed into an enormous red-skinned alien. He was so big he could barely fit in the back of The Rust Bucket.

'Great,' he muttered. '*Now* I turn into Four Arms!'

❈ ❈ ❈

In their hideout under the Thirty-Ninth Street bridge, a familiar gang of boys were having the

worst night of their lives. They scrambled away
from Kevin, trying to avoid the fireballs
he hurled at them.

'Kevin, we can work this out!' begged
the leader.

'I don't think so,' Kevin snarled. With a
blast of his heat powers he brought a section of
the bridge crashing down. It landed on top
of the gang, trapping them underneath.

Kevin raised his arm and pointed it
towards the trapped boys. An evil smile crept
across his face.

'So much for your gang!'

With a sudden **WHOOSH**, Kevin's
Heatblast energy faded away, leaving him
normal once again. He stared down at his
hands, confused.

'What's going on?' he demanded.

'Your power's gone,' boomed a voice
from behind him. Four Arms landed on the
concrete, cracking it into pieces.

'Looks like you're about to give me some more, Ben.'

'No.'

Kevin leaped up on to the fallen rubble and held his hands over the heads of the gang members. Energy crackled from his palms.

'You don't have a choice,' Kevin smirked. 'I've still got enough juice to fry these guys.'

Four Arms stepped forwards and

snatched Kevin up before he could hurt anyone. He didn't realise he'd walked right into his enemy's trap.

Kevin pressed his hands against the alien's arms and felt a wave of energy surge through his body. He laughed as he soaked up Ben's alien power. He could feel himself getting stronger with every second that passed.

He threw an elbow back, smashing Four Arms in the face. The alien released his grip, letting the boy slide to the ground. When Kevin stood back up, he had transformed into a twisted version of the four-armed red giant.

Roaring, Kevin thundered forwards. As he ran, another pair of arms sprouted from his shoulders! He drew one back and lashed out with a punch. It caught Four Arms under the chin and set him crashing through a stack of concrete blocks.

Kevin cracked all six sets of knuckles at once. 'This is gonna be real fun!'

'Tell me about it,' Four Arms replied, getting back to his feet.

He ducked, avoiding a flurry of wild punches from Kevin. Moving fast, Four Arms caught his opponent by the wrists, and the two giants began to grapple each other.

'I'm taking all your alien powers!' Kevin

growled. His two extra arms caught Four Arms by the throat and slammed him hard against a wall. While the alien was still dazed, Kevin jerked him off the ground, then drove his head down into the concrete.

Up on the bridge, Grandpa and Gwen leaped from The Rust Bucket and rushed down to where the fight was taking place. There was nothing they could do to help Ben – Kevin was too strong, but they could help the trapped gang.

'Moving day,' Grandpa told them as he cleared away the rubble. 'Get out!'

The gang didn't need telling twice. Not daring to look back, they all took to their heels and fled into the night.

A moment later, a flailing mass of limbs hit the side of the bridge like a cannonball. Kevin and Four Arms were locked in battle, each driving powerful punches into their opponent.

Without warning, the Omnitrix started to flash and **_BLEEP!_** Four Arms stared at it in horror. The transformation was about to wear off!

Realising he had no time to lose, he gave it everything he had. Fast, furious punches rained down on Kevin's head, dazing him. Four Arms slammed his feet against Kevin's chest. As the six-armed mutant staggered backwards, Four Arms followed up with a devastating shoulder-slam. It flipped Kevin end over end, and sent him crashing into one of the bridge's support pillars.

'C'mon, I give. I give. I'm sorry!' Kevin wailed, struggling to get free of a mound of rubble that had collapsed on to him. 'Please, just lighten up!'

'I just did,' announced Ben, who was now back in human form. 'By about three hundred pounds.'

'Guess I just went too wild with power,' whimpered Kevin. 'I don't have anyone else like you to help me.'

'We can still be partners,' Ben offered. 'We'd just be kicking butt for good instead of for ourselves.'

Kevin considered this. 'What's in it for me?'

'For starters, people will like you.' Ben

stretched out his hand. Kevin stared at it for
a long time, before reaching out to accept the
offer of friendship.

Or so Ben thought. Instead of shaking his
hand, Kevin grabbed Ben by the wrist and lifted
him so his feet were dangling in mid-air.

'Oh, man! You are so dim,' Kevin
cackled. 'Now give me the watch!' He took

hold of the Omnitrix and gave it a tug. It was stuck fast.

'You're the one who's dim. I told you I can't take it off!'

Kevin gave the watch another pull. As he did, a bolt of bright green energy surged from inside the device. The blast launched them both in opposite directions. Ben hurtled safely into his grandpa's arms, while Kevin smashed through another bridge support. With a hideous grinding of concrete and metal, the bridge crumpled and collapsed on top of him.

When Kevin pulled himself free, he no longer had six arms. He didn't even have four. Instead, he was back to being his old self – something he wasn't too pleased about at all.

'Nooo!' he screamed, and then, before anyone could stop him, he turned and fled into the dark back alleys of the city.

'I'm sorry, Grandpa,' said Ben. 'For everything.'

Grandpa Max nodded solemnly. 'I know you are. You're my grandson, and nothing will ever change that.' He turned away and walked back towards The Rust Bucket. 'But my trust is something you'll have to earn back.'

Ben watched his grandpa go. He'd learned a lot about trust today. He'd prove to Grandpa Max that he was trustworthy, even if it took all summer.

✖ ✖ ✖

In an abandoned subway station, a misshapen figure sat hidden by shadow. He could feel something happening to him. Something was changing.

'If they thought I was a freak before,' Kevin hissed, 'just wait!'

As a flickering flame sprung up from his hand, Kevin laughed. The sound echoed around the station before being swallowed forever by the darkness.